Norse, of Course!
The Roots of Yggdrasil

Author: N.K. Stoner

Author:
N.K. Stoner

Illustrated by:
Kristin Stoner

Graphic Editor,
Layout and Design:
Samantha Stoner

www.Norhalla.com

Norse are the people
In stories of old
Sagas and Eddas
Their history unfolds

Thousands of years
In a time long ago
Our people lived
With more to be told

The Aesir and Vanir
Revered ancestors they be
Remnants of their lives
Lost to history

Odin did ponder
The Aesir-Vanir war
"What were we missing?
Could there be more?"

At the conclusion
Of the great war
Kvasir was mediator
To settle the score

Agreements were made
With importance indeed
Both sides shook hands
Then shared in some mead

For the treaty to last
It was written down
Poetry the language
Kvasir it found

Odin reflects
Remembers the day
As part of the truce
Freyja came to stay

Odur saw her beauty
And caught in her gaze
Overwhelmed he was
His thoughts in a haze

Confident and sure
Beautiful and pleased
She introduced herself
"Teacher to thee"

She introduced the Aesir
To the splendor of seid
Being touched in one's soul
Is how relationships are made

Freyja taught also
Of the soul mate too
How to evolve the soul
And ascend as two

Her place in Asgard
Established in trust
Head of the Valkyrie
High Priestess as such

Odin further reflects
On Aesir ways
How spiritual Vanir
Also have their place

Vili had been sent
To live with the Vanir
Copy their books
And send them back here

Delivered by Norns
Vanir priestesses three
Sat down with Odin
Answered questions for he

Odin deciphered
Vanir books he did read
Their ways are different
But invaluable indeed

Vanir women known
To fight alongside the men
From an age very young
To protect and defend

To read and to write
Men and women alike
To council together
Decisions made right

Spiritual ascension
Was in their thoughts
By all Vanir people
Divine knowledge was sought

Upon seeing the books
Vanir history in form
Odin was piqued
And sought to learn more

Odin did recognize
Need of more teaching
Vanir in its care
Well of Urd ever-reaching

A temple was built
Three Norns in charge
To teach and dispense
Justice to discharge

The priestesses three
Urd, Verdani, and Skuld
To teach Vanir ways
Norse future to mold

Taught to the women
Medicine and Seid
How to be Shield Maidens
And ways to do trade

Odin was pleased
He visited the Well
Norse people learning
The future will tell

Odin immersed
In deep absorbed thoughts
Thinks of Vergelmir Well
And knowledge it brought

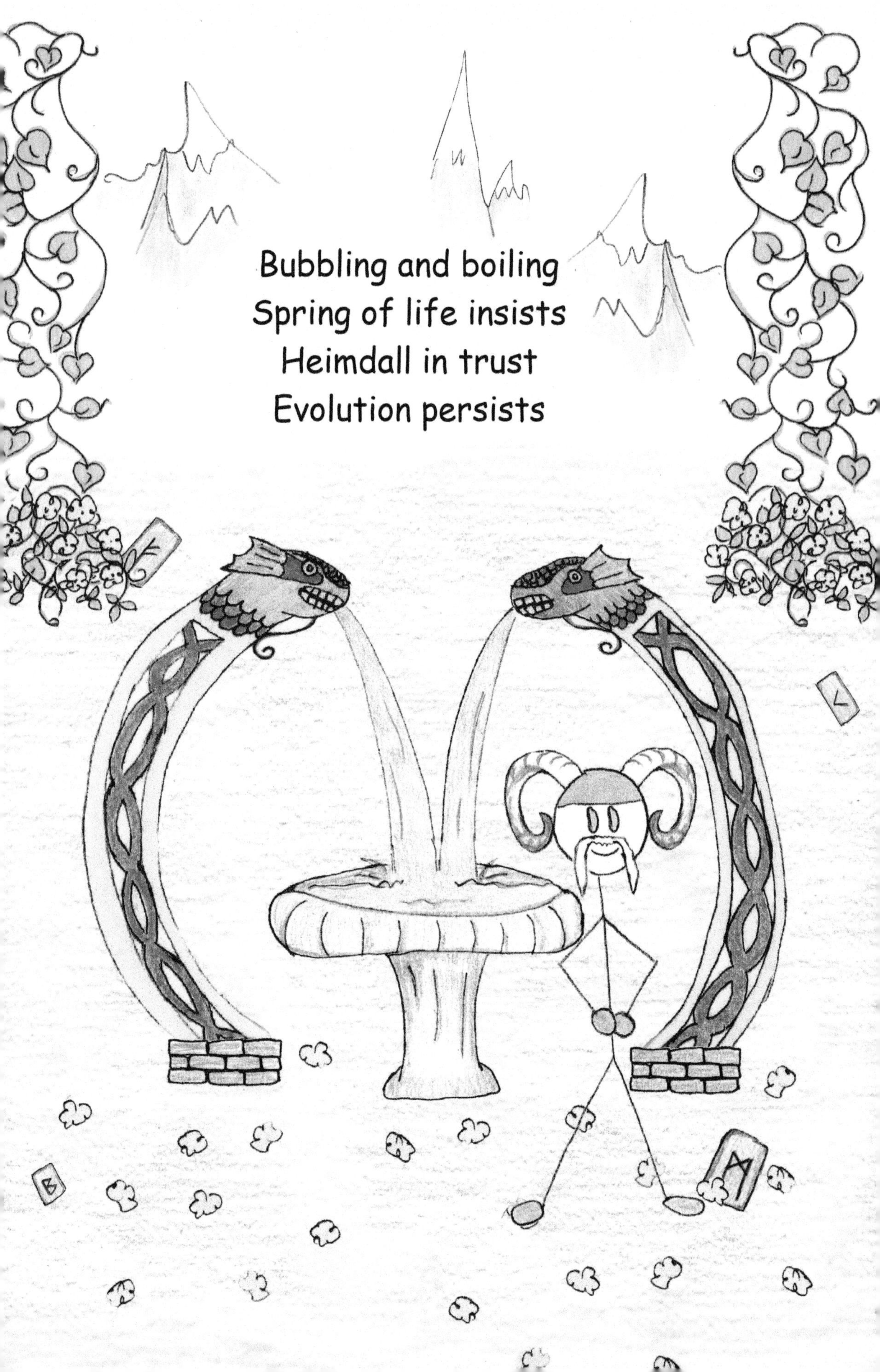
Bubbling and boiling
Spring of life insists
Heimdall in trust
Evolution persists

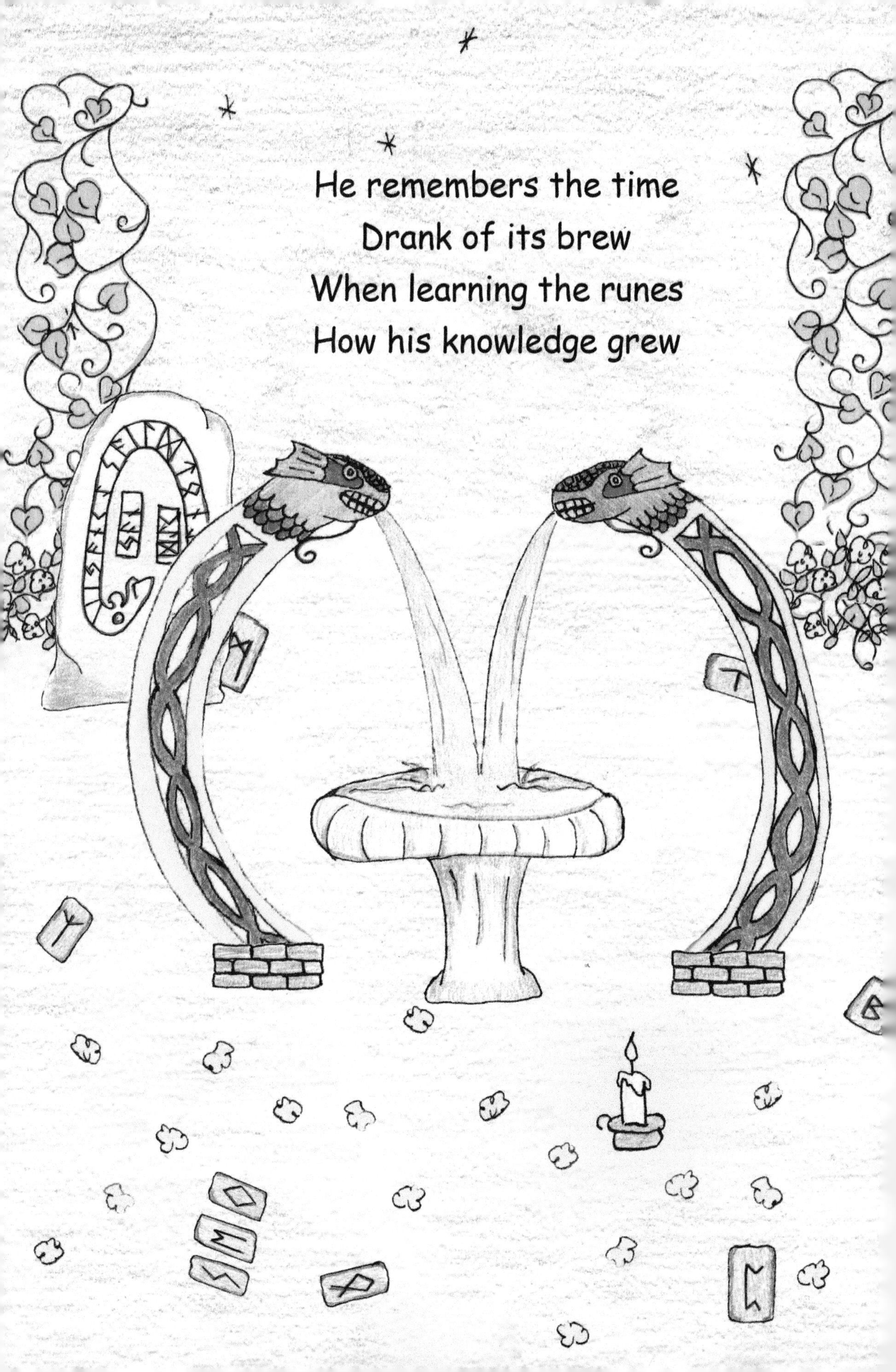
He remembers the time
Drank of its brew
When learning the runes
How his knowledge grew

He struggled and suffered
Nine moons it did take
Runes he did learn
With nary a break

Reading and writing
The foundation of all
To speak to the future
Prophesy does call

His thoughts came in focus
And settled again
Reflected on Mimir
Philosopher friend

Visits he had
To the Well of Mimir
Wisdom was gained
Through sacrifice not fear

Knowledge not free
A price must be paid
Not Mimir's rules
But Nature made

Nature does teach
Through simple instruction
Put your hand in the fire
Lesson 1 introduction

If all that was learned
Is the fire is wrong
The lesson therein
Can be lost lifelong

If fire is wrong
You don't use the tool
Now starving to death
Who is the fool?

The purpose of pain
Nature does teach
Learn the right lessons
Mental discipline to reach

Odin considered
Vast knowledge learned
All the great Wells
Feeding the Norse yearn

Knowledge the Wells have
And lessons they teach
Made into Laws
All realms to reach

Contemplated he did
On what they should be
He settled his thoughts
On the first three

Reading and Writing
Runes all must learn
Evolution the key
Door to the future it turns

Warriors trained all
In body and mind
Viewpoint to battle
Fear not to find

Spiritual ascension
All must be taught
Soul mate to choose
Odur to be sought

Both men and women
By Odin's decree
All Norse shall live
By these Laws three

As leader of Asgard
And all people Norse
His burden therein
New laws to enforce

Education and knowledge
The task at hand
To be ever prosperous
Yggdrasil demands

Freyja insisted
And Odin agreed
These ways must be taught
To all Norse under the tree

Odin's Law did encompass
The ways of Vanir
Blended with Aesir
To be Norse far and near

Runes Game

Learn the runes on the following page.

Spelling and reading in runes is done using phonetics, meaning that words are spelled like they sound.

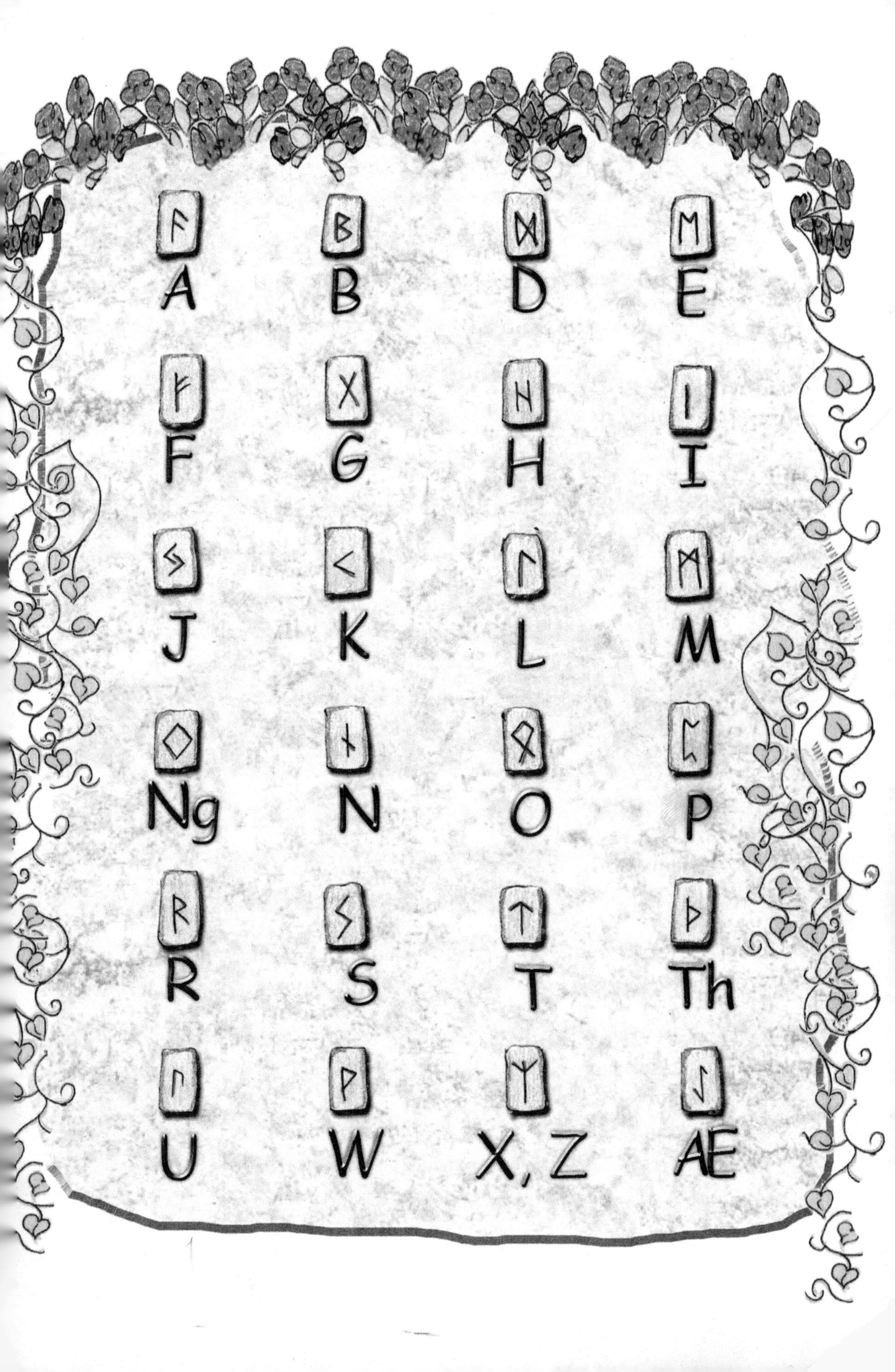
A
B
D
E
F
G
H
I
J
K
L
M
Ng
N
O
P
R
S
T
Th
U
W
X, Z
Æ

Name Game

Buri ᛒᚢᚱᛁ
Freki ᚠᚱᛖᚲᛁ
Freyja ᚠᚱᛖᛃᚨ
Freyr ᚠᚱᛖᚱ
Frigga ᚠᚱᛁᚷᚷᚨ
Geri ᚷᛖᚱᛁ
Gullinbursti ᚷᚢᛚᛚᛁᚾᛒᚢᚱᛊᛏᛁ
Heimdall ᚺᛖᛁᛗᛞᚨᛚᛚ
Hugin ᚺᚢᚷᛁᚾ
Idunna ᛁᛞᚢᚾᚾᚨ
Kvasir ᚲᚹᚨᛊᛁᚱ
Loki ᛚᛟᚲᛁ

Mimir ᛗᛁᛗᛁᚱ
Munnin ᛗᚢᚾᚾᛁᚾ
Njord ᚾᛃᛟᚱᛞ
Odin ᛟᚦᛁᚾ
Sif ᛊᛁᚠ
Skadi ᛊᚲᚨᛞᛁ
Skuld ᛊᚲᚢᛚᛞ
Sleipnir ᛊᛚᛖᛁᛈᚾᛁᚱ
Thor ᚦᛟᚱ
Tyr ᛏᛁᚱ
Urd ᚢᚱᛞ
Ve ᚹᛖ
Verdani ᚹᛖᚱᛞᚨᚾᛁ
Vili ᚹᛁᛚᛁ

Find their names in runes on the following pages

ᚠᚱᛖᚲᛁ
ᚺᛖᛁ
ᛗᛞᚨ
ᛚᛚᚱ
ᛁᚱ
ᚦᛁᛚᛁ
ᚠᚱᛁᚷᚷᚨ

ᛁᛞᚢᚾᚾᚨ
ᛋᛁᚠ
ᚦᛟᚱ
ᛚᛟᚲᛁ
ᚠᚱᛖᛃᚨ
ᛗᛁᛗᛁᚱ

Pronunciation Guide

Aesir = [**ay**-sir] said like "ace + sir"
rhymes with "racer"

Asgard = [**az**-gard] said like "az + guard"

Bergelmir = [**ber**-gil-meer]
said like "burr + gill + mere"

Bifrost = [**bi**-frost] said like "by + frost"

Buri = [**bur**-ee] rhymes with "blurry"

Edda = [**ed**-uh] rhymes with "data"

Freki = [**fre**-kee] said like "fre + key"

Freyja = [**fray**-yah] said like "fray + ya"

Freyr = [**fray**] said like "fray" rhymes with "say"

Frigga = [**frig**-uh] rhymes with "twig" + "uh"

Geri = [**je**-ree] said like "jerry"

Gullinbursti = [**gull**-in-bur-stee]
said like "gull + in + bur + stee"

Heimdall = [**hime**-dal] said like "hime + doll"

Hugin = [**hew**-gen] rhymes with "again"

Idunna = [i-**doo**-na] said like "eye + do + na"

Jotun = [**yo**-ten] said like "yo + ten"

Kvasir = [**kvahs**-eer] said like "ka + vas + er"

Loki = [**lo**-kee] said like "low + key"

Mimir = [**mim**-eer] said like "mim + ear"

Munnin = [**mew**-nen] said like "mew + nin"

Njord = [**nee**-yord] said like "knee + y-ord"
rhymes with "cord"

Norn = [**norn**] rhymes with "thorn"

Odin = [**oh**-din] said like "O + den"

Saga = [**sah**-guh] rhymes with "lava"

Seid = [**say**-d] rhymes with "made"

Sif = [**sif**] rhymes with "jif"

Skadi = [skah-**dee**] rhymes with "muddy"

Skuld = [**skuld**] said like "skull + d"

Sleipnir = [**slip**-near] said like "slip + near"

Svadilfare = [**svah**-dill-fare] "svad" rhymes with "glad"
said like "svad + dill + fare"

Thor = [**thor**] rhymes with "more"

Tyr = [**teer**] rhymes with "clear"

rd = [**urd**] rhymes with "word"

alkyire = [**val**-keer-ee] said like "val + keer + ee"

anir = [**vah**-neer] said like "veneer"

e = [**vay**] rhymes with "say"

erdani = [ver-**dan**-ee] said like "ver + dan + ee"

ergelmir = [**ver**-gill-meer] said like "ver + gill + meer"

ili = [**vill**-ee] rhymes with "silly"

ggdrasil = [**ig**-dra-sil] said like "ig + dra + sill"

mir = [**yim**-yeer] said like "yim + year"

CPSIA information can be obtained at www.ICGtesting.com
Printed in the USA
BVOW10s1046250216

437869BV00021B/241/P

9 781941 442050